S0-DZD-844

This Book Belongs To

_____

Kramer Makes David Smile
Copyright © 2010 by Donald E. Sexauer. All rights reserved.

This title is also available as a Tate Out Loud product. Visit www.tatepublishing.com for more information.

No part of this publication may be reproduced, stored in a retrieval system or transmitted in any way by any means, electronic, mechanical, photocopy, recording or otherwise without the prior permission of the author except as provided by USA copyright law.

The opinions expressed by the author are not necessarily those of Tate Publishing, LLC.

Published by Tate Publishing & Enterprises, LLC
127 E. Trade Center Terrace | Mustang, Oklahoma 73064 USA
1.888.361.9473 | www.tatepublishing.com

Tate Publishing is committed to excellence in the publishing industry. The company reflects the philosophy established by the founders, based on Psalm 68:11,
"The Lord gave the word and great was the company of those who published it."

Book design copyright © 2010 by Tate Publishing, LLC. All rights reserved.
Cover and interior design by Chris Webb
Illustrations by Donald E. Sexauer

Published in the United States of America

ISBN: 978-1-61739-333-4
1. Juvenile Fiction / Social Issues / Emotions & Feelings
2. Ages 4-8
10.11.23

Kramer Makes David Smile

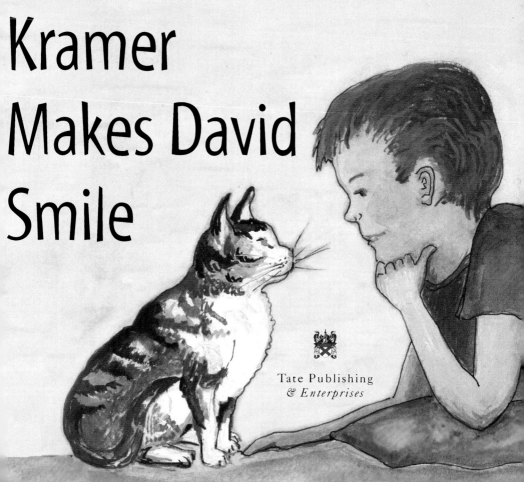

Tate Publishing
& Enterprises

written & illustrated by Donald E. Sexauer

David never seemed to smile!

His mother asked, "David, why do always have a moue on your face?" His Mother said "moue" like a moo that cows make. David never mooed like a cow.

So, Jenna guessed that a moue was when David's bottom lip stuck out and his mouth went down…the opposite of a smile.

David never answered. But he stuck his bottom lip out farther.

And he did not smile!

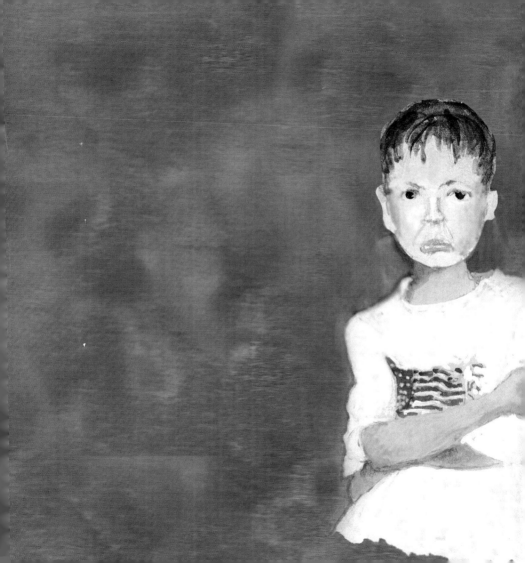

David, age 6, lived with his brother Jack, age 9, in a house with his father and mother.

They had a dog named Jenna who enjoyed the house. She was young and easy to please. And they had a cat named Kramer, who put up with the house. He was old, almost 16 years old. And was wise beyond his years.

He really liked living with Megan, the mother. He had lived with Megan when she was single.

David thought life could be better.

Kramer *knew* his life should be better.

They looked at each other balefully: *Perhaps*, they both thought, *he knows what I'm thinking.*

The house was not the problem.

The two-story house stood in the middle of a hill and was sheltered by it. The north side looked up at the hill; the south side looked down to a valley.

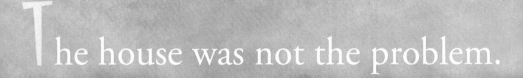

There, children played lacrosse or soccer supervised by father coaches teaching them how to play. When the children went home, grown-ups brought their dogs to run joyfully around, chasing balls and retrieving them or just letting the dogs run free from their leashes.

David liked his house all right,
he had to admit it. It certainly was big!

So he walked through his home and thought about what he did.

The first floor had a living room where he did legos. And he liked the fireplace in the winter.

And a dining room where
he did jig saw puzzles on the big table.

And a kitchen where he looked out the window and ate his Cheerios at breakfast time at a granite counter.

And a family room, which also had a fireplace, and where he could go outside through the sliding door.

There were other rooms, too. But these were the ones David really used.

Kramer followed David around and thought, *Yes, it is a big house, but it had one place that was almost entirely mine.*

The cellar! One whole side was above ground because of the hill. Kramer loved to sit by the sliding door and look out at the birds and other things. *And I can go out all by myself! David can't.*

The problem for both David and Kramer was they felt incomplete.

Why didn't they feel happy? What was happiness, anyway?

So David began to think

of the things he did during the day.

David enjoyed drawing. Kramer enjoyed watching David draw. But he often fell asleep.

David liked painting.

Kramer liked it less because he often was
splashed with the paint.

David did not like to be bossed by Jack.

In fact, Kramer often had nightmares of Jack taking the paints way from David "to show David how to paint." In the process Kramer had paint splashed all over him.

Kramer thought David should get used to it.

After all, Kramer got bossed by everyone.

And only Kramer was covered with paint!

A family activity outside of the house was Jack's game playing. David was brought to every game that Jack played: swimming meets, soccer games, and lacrosse games. Jack excelled in all games he played.

He won praise, awards and even some medals for swimming.

But David liked lacrosse the best…maybe because he could see Jack so perfectly in his helmet, his face cage, the padding, and the stick. He loved the equipment.

He felt a moue come automatically over his mouth.

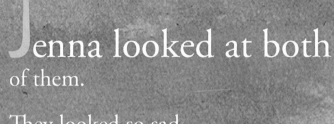

Jenna looked at both of them.

They looked so sad.

She wondered why … for a little while.
Then she began wagging her tail.

Still...

something was missing. Both Kramer and David felt there had to be something more!

One day when Jack was in school and his mother was working upstairs, David gazed out the family room window that looked into the backyard.

The tree leaves had turned color from the clear, cool October air.

In the middle of a very green lawn walked Kramer, sniffing the brisk air.

He almost looked happy.

He looked happy when he stretched out in the sun. Happier when he rolled on the grass. Ecstatic when he ran into the woods, his tail disappearing in the undergrowth.

David had to wonder if Kramer was happy just being out there in the sun?

Puzzled, he looked at his easel and paints and the drawing he had started. *I really have fun doing this. I think it even makes me happy.*

He looked at the granite countertop where he had his meals. He thought, *I like eating my cheerios and drinking milk. I might even be happy doing that. I certainly enjoy pushing the Cheerios into patterns in my bowl.*

A loud *meow* made David

turn to the sliding door. Kramer wanted to come in and eat. He looked all puffed up from the outdoors.

David slid the door open. Kramer came in with his tail swishing about. He started rubbing against David's legs. He purred so loudly David felt pleased — no, happy!

David felt his mouth relax and turn up at the ends! Where had the moue gone? David filled a bowl with cat food and knelt down to give it to Kramer, who practically knocked him over with glee. David patted Kramer's head as Kramer ate.

"You know, Kramer, you really taught me something today."

Kramer purred and looked into David's face.

"You really enjoy what you have…and so will I." Kramer continued to purr. "I'm going to be just like you!"

He stood up. "I'm going to have fun with what I have and try to forget what I don't have. And Jack is a good brother. I am going to enjoy those games and try to be as good a player as Jack—maybe even better." He went to his drawing and smiled.

Kramer thought David had a
great idea. He'd do the same thing from now on.

Meanwhile, he'd just eat his food. Talk about enjoying what you have!

Mmmmm. Good.

He would be more content after he finished eating.

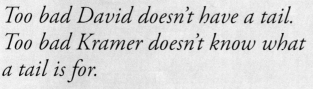

Jenna looked at them both.

She even let her tongue hang out! *It's about time they realized how much fun life is.*

Too bad David doesn't have a tail.
Too bad Kramer doesn't know what
a tail is for.

But that's life, and it's wonderful.
Especially since I have a tail.

And it's wagging.
Why not?

One day, when Jack, David, and the father were playing catch with the lacrosse sticks, Jenna realized that she never heard Megan talk to David about his moue. He smiled a lot now.

Smiling just happens when you let it. Like wagging your tail!

The End

listen|imagine|view|experience

AUDIO BOOK DOWNLOAD INCLUDED WITH THIS BOOK!

In your hands you hold a complete digital entertainment package. In addition to the paper version, you receive a free download of the audio version of this book. Simply use the code listed below when visiting our website. Once downloaded to your computer, you can listen to the book through your computer's speakers, burn it to an audio CD or save the file to your portable music device (such as Apple's popular iPod) and listen on the go!

How to get your free audio book digital download:

1. Visit www.tatepublishing.com and click on the e|LIVE logo on the home page.
2. Enter the following coupon code:
   daa7-663d-ba6d-f7a1-7408-8f3c-0ce0-3f99
3. Download the audio book from your e|LIVE digital locker and begin enjoying your new digital entertainment package today!